THE NONSENSE SHOW

Dedicated to Joanna Carey

For **René Magritte**, the Belgian surrealist artist who famously painted a realistic pipe and wrote underneath *"Ceci n'est pas une pipe."* (This is not a pipe.)

Ann Beneduce, Consulting Editor. Ms. Beneduce has been Eric Carle's editor since his first books, *1, 2, 3, to the Zoo* and *The Very Hungry Caterpillar.*

Eric Carle **THE NONSENSE SHOW**

PUFFIN

Welcome, friends!
Don't be slow.
Step right up to
The Nonsense Show!

"I'm too wet!" said the Bird.
"I can't fly! It's absurd!"

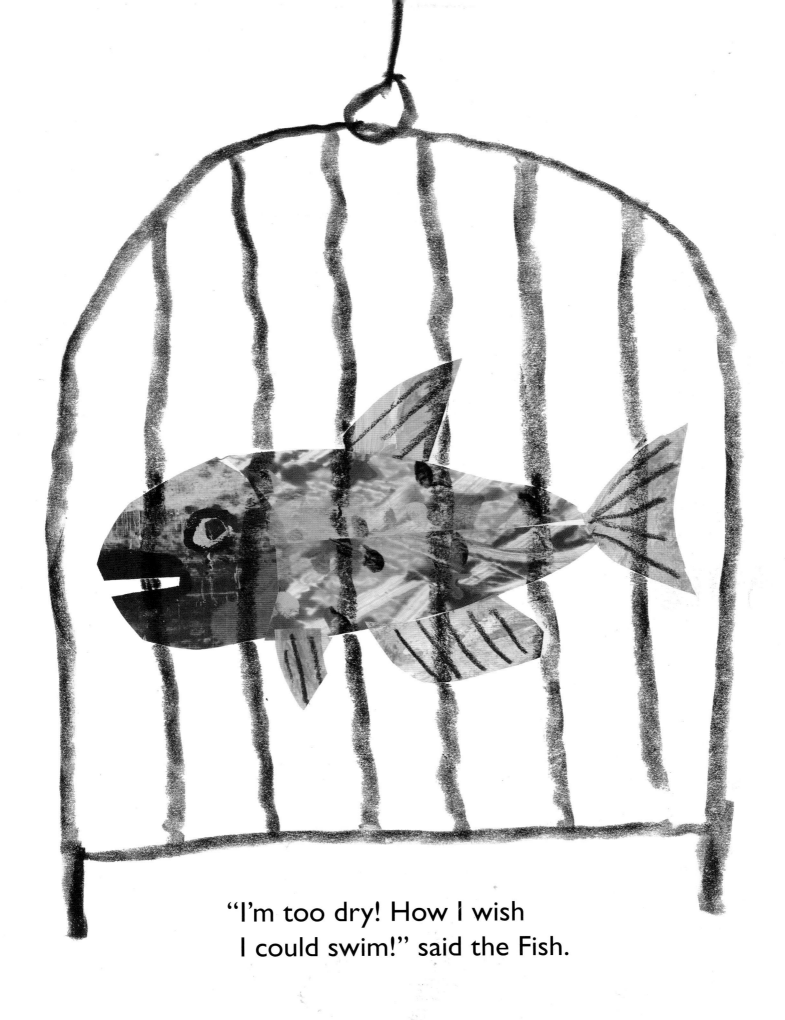

"I'm too dry! How I wish
I could swim!" said the Fish.

"Ouch!
Who's that in my pouch?"

"I'm s-s-seeking my tail,
Can you see where it's gone?"
His-s-sed snake number one.

"What a coincidence!—
Mine's missing, too!"
His-s-sed snake number two.

"I am supposed to catch YOU!"
 Meowed the cat.
"Yes," squeaked the mouse.
"Of course, that's true
 But you must know...
 We're in a Nonsense Show!"

Oh, dear! Look here:
It says, "NO GAS!"
Alas!

No gas?
Don't worry,
We're not in a hurry!

What a funny-looking ball
Thought the tennis ace

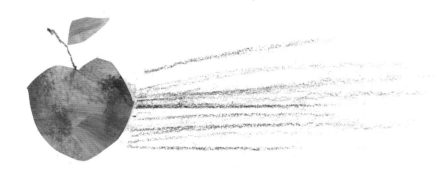

And wound up
With applesauce
In her face.

One sheep,
Two sheep,
Three sheep,
Four,
And after that
How many more?
Z-z-z-z-z-z-z-z

KO!

Get out of my house!
Said the dog.
"But where can I go?"
Barked the man.
"For all that I care
You can fly to the moon,
But go soon."

And that's why
We've now got
A man in the moon!
Believe it or not...

Up-sy,
Down-sy,
Nice
And
Straight.

Smile
A
Mile...

Bravo! That's Great!

Who's that I see?
It can't be me.
I'll tell you who
It looks like: *You!*

"Let's trade hats,"
The rider said,
But, "Neigh, neigh!"
Said the horse.

"Let's trade heads
 Instead, okay?"
 And so they did,
 Of course.

"Hurry up!" said BOTTOM.
"Wait for me!" said TOP.
But they couldn't agree,
So they never did stop.

Could a leopard
Change his spot
To a tiger-ish stripe?
Probably not.

Would a tiger wish
To swap his stripe
For a leopard's spot?
Certainly not!

Why is Mr. Up up,
Why is Mrs. Down down?

It's not a mistake,
It's just how they eat cake.

This yellow rubber duck I found
Has feet for walking on the ground,
But don't you think that this duck *ought-er*
Get webbed feet to swim in water?

PUFFIN BOOKS
UK | USA | Canada | Ireland | Australia | India | New Zealand | South Africa
Puffin Books is part of the Penguin Random House group of companies whose addresses
can be found at global.penguinrandomhouse.com

First published in the USA by Philomel Books,
an imprint of Penguin Young Readers Group, 2015
Published in Great Britain by Puffin Books 2015

001

Copyright © Eric Carle, 2015

The moral right of the author/illustrator has been asserted

Text set in 22-point Gill Sans Regular
The art was created with painted tissue-paper collage

A CIP catalogue record for this book is available from the British Library

Printed in China

ISBN: 978–0–141–36513–8

Eric Carle's name and his signature logotype are trademarks of Eric Carle

To find out more about Eric Carle and his books, please visit **eric-carle.com**
To learn about The Eric Carle Museum of Picture Book Art, please visit **carlemuseum.org**